M
Co.

Chinese Graded Reader

Breakthough Level: 150 Characters

我的老师是火星人

Wǒ de Lǎoshī Shì Huǒxīngrén

My Teacher Is a Martian

by John Pasden and Jared Turner

Mind Spark Press LLC

SHANGHAI

Published by Mind Spark Press LLC

Shanghai, China

Mandarin Companion is a trademark of Mind Spark Press LLC.

Copyright © Mind Spark Press LLC, 2019

For information about educational or bulk purchases, please contact
Mind Spark Press at business@mandarincompanion.com.

Instructor and learner resources and traditional Chinese editions of
the Mandarin Companion series are available
at www.MandarinCompanion.com.

First paperback print edition 2019

Library of Congress Cataloging-in-Publication Data
Turner, Jared.

My Teacher Is a Martian : Mandarin Companion Graded Readers: Level 0,
Simplified Chinese Edition / John Pasden and Jared Turner; [edited by] John
Pasden, Chen Shishuang, Li Jiong, Ma Lihua

1st paperback edition.

Shanghai, China / Salt Lake City, UT: Mind Spark Press LLC, 2019

Library of Congress Control Number: 2019910036
ISBN: 9781941875490 (Paperback)
ISBN: 9781941875513 (Paperback/traditional ch)
ISBN: 9781941875506 (ebook)
ISBN: 9781941875520 (ebook/traditional ch)
MCID: SFH20190722T170053JT

Mandarin Companion Graded Readers

Now you can read books in Chinese that are fun and help accelerate language learning. Every book in the Mandarin Companion series is carefully written to use characters, words, and grammar that a learner is likely to know.

The Mandarin Companion Leveling System has been meticulously developed through an in-depth stastical analysis of textbooks and education programs. Each story is written in a style that is fun and easy to understand so that you improve as you read.

Mandarin Companion Breakthrough Level

The Breakthrough Level is intended for Chinese learners who have obtained a low elementary or novice level of Chinese. Most students will be able to approach this book after one year of traditional formal study, depending on the learner and program. In creating this story, we have carefully balanced the need for level-appropriate simplicity against the needs of the story's plot.

The Breakthrough Level is written using a core set of 150 characters, a subset of the 300 characters used in Mandarin Companion Level 1. This ensures that the vocabulary will be limited to simple, everyday words, composed of characters that the learner is most likely to know. Any new characters used outside of the 150 Breakthrough Level characters are exclusively borrowed from the Level 1 character set, meaning that with each new story, the reader is systematically building toward Level 1.

Key words that the reader is not likely to know are added gradually over the course of the story accompanied by a numbered footnote for each instance. Pinyin and an English definition are provided at the bottom of the page for the first instance of each key word, and a complete glossary is provided at the back of the book. All proper nouns have been underlined to help the reader distinguish between names and other words.

What level is right for me?

If you are able to comfortably read this book without looking up lots of words, then this book is likely at your level. It is ideal to have at most only one unknown word or character for every 40-50 words or characters that are read.

Once you are able to read fluidly and quickly without interruption you are ready for the next level. Even if you are able to understand all of the words in the book, we recommend that readers build fluidity and reading speed before moving to higher levels.

How will this help my Chinese?

Reading extensively in a language you are learning is one of the most effective ways to build fluency. However, the key is to read at a high level of comprehension. Reading at the appropriate level in Chinese will increase your speed of character recognition, help you to acquire vocabulary faster, teach you to naturally learn grammar, and train your brain to think in Chinese. It also makes learning Chinese more fun and enjoyable. You will experience the sense of accomplishment and confidence that only comes from reading entire books in Chinese.

Extensive Reading

After years of studying Chinese, many people ask, "why can't I become fluent in Chinese?" Fluency can only happen when the language enters our "comfort zone." This comfort comes after significant exposure to and experience with the language. The more times you meet a word, phrase, or grammar point the more readily it will enter your comfort zone.

In the world of language research, experts agree that learners can acquire new vocabulary through reading only if the overall text can be understood. Decades of research indicate that if we know approximately 98% of the words in a book, we can comfortably "pick up" the 2% that is unfamiliar. Reading at this 98% comprehension level is referred to as "extensive reading."

Research in extensive reading has shown that it accelerates vocabulary learning and helps the learner to naturally understand grammar. Perhaps most importantly, it trains the brain to automatically recognize familiar language, thereby freeing up mental energy to focus on meaning and ideas. As they build reading speed and fluency, learners will move from reading "word by word" to processing "chunks of language." A defining feature is that it's less painful than the "intensive reading" commonly used in textbooks. In fact, extensive reading can be downright fun.

Graded Readers

Graded readers are the best books for learners to "extensively" read. Research has taught us that learners need to "encounter" a word 10-30 times before truly learning it, and often many more times for particularly complicated or abstract words. Graded readers are appropriate for learners because the language is controlled and simplified, as opposed to the language in native texts, which is inevitably difficult and often demotivating. Reading extensively with graded readers allows learners to bring together all of the language they have studied and absorb how the words naturally work together.

To become fluent, learners must not only understand the meaning of a word, but also understand its nuances, how to use it in conversation, how to pair it with other words, where it fits into natural word order, and how it is used in grammar structures. No textbook could ever be written to teach all of this explicitly. When used properly, a textbook introduces the language and provides the basic meanings, while graded readers consolidate, strengthen, and deepen understanding.

Without graded readers, learners would have to study dictionaries, textbooks, sample dialogs, and simple conversations until they have randomly encountered enough Chinese for it to enter their comfort zones. With proper use of graded readers, learners can tackle this issue and develop greater fluency now, at their current levels, instead of waiting until some period in the distant future. With a stronger foundation and greater confidence at their current levels, learners are encouraged and motivated to continue their Chinese studies to even greater heights. Plus, they'll quickly learn that reading Chinese is fun!

About Mandarin Companion

Mandarin Companion was started by Jared Turner and John Pasden who met one fateful day on a bus in Shanghai when the only remaining seat left them sitting next to each other. A year later, Jared had greatly improved his Chinese using extensive reading but was frustrated at the lack of suitable reading materials. He approached John with the prospect of creating their own series. Having worked in Chinese education for nearly a decade, John was intrigued with the idea and thus began the Mandarin Companion series.

John majored in Japanese in college, but started learning Mandarin and later moved to China where his learning accelerated. After developing language proficiency, he was admitted into an all-Chinese masters program in applied linguistics at East China Normal University in Shanghai. Throughout his learning process, John developed an open mind to different learning styles and a tendency to challenge conventional wisdom in the field of teaching Chinese. He has since worked at ChinesePod as academic director and host, and opened his own consultancy, AllSet Learning, in Shanghai to help individuals acquire Chinese language proficiency. He lives in Shanghai with his wife and children.

After graduate school and with no Chinese language skills, Jared decided to move to China with his young family in search of career opportunities. Later while working on an investment project, Jared learned about extensive reading and decided that if it was as effective as it claimed to be, it could help him learn Chinese. In three months, he read 10 Chinese graded readers and his language ability quickly improved from speaking words and phrases to a conversational level. Jared has an MBA from Purdue University and a bachelor in Economics from the University of Utah. He lives in Shanghai with his wife and children.

Credits

Original Author: Jared Turner

Story Authors: John Pasden, Jared Turner

Editor-in-Chief: John Pasden

Content Editor: Chen Shishuang

Editors: Li Jiong, Ma Lihua

Illustrator: Hu Sheng

Producer: Jared Turner

Acknowledgments

We are grateful to Li Jiong, Ma Lihua, Song Shen, Tan Rong, Chen Shishuang, and the entire team at AllSet Learning for working on this project and contributing the perfect mix of talent to produce this series.

Special thanks to Wang Hui and her 7th grade Chinese dual immersion class at Adele C. Young Intermediate School for being our test readers: AJ Bushnell, Brandon Murray, Colin Grunander, Emma Page, Isaak Diehl, Jackson Faerber, Jason Lee, Kyden Cefalo, Max Norton, Maxwell Isaacson, Olivia Barker, and Xavier Putnam. Also thanks to Jake Liu, Paris Yamamoto, Rory O'Neill, and Miles Turner for being our test readers.

Table of Contents

Story Adaptation Notes

Any learner that has managed to learn 150 Chinese characters knows it is not an easy task, and the prospect of reading a real text in Chinese seems discouragingly faroff. Typically textbook dialogs are the only reading material available for years on end. That's why being able to read an actual story with only 150 Chinese characters is a very big deal, and a huge help to the fluency development of early-stage learners.

The stories told at this 150-character Breakthrough Level are special, however. Nouns, verbs amd adjectives at this level are in short supply, and the stories revolve around the limited vocabulary by necessity. This is why Breakthrough Level stories are not adaptations of western classics. They are original stories co-written by John Pasden and Jared Turner, specifically designed to be engaging to readers despite the limitations.

When John and Jared were generating story ideas at the Breakthrough Level, the character for "fire," 火 (huǒ), and for "star," 星 (xīng), were on a sheet of possible characters to be used. Together, these characters form the Chinese word for Mars: 火星 (Huǒxīng), and set off the quest to create a sci-fi story using the Chinese name of the fourth planet in our solar system. Jared recalled reading a story called "My Teacher is an Alien" in his youth, which provided the inspiration for a story about two Chinese elementary school students who suspect their teacher is, in fact, from Mars. From this genesis of an idea, the Mandarin Companion story *My Teacher is a Martian* was born. For those who can read this book at an enjoyable pace, you are already well on your way towards progressing to the Level 1 stories.

P.S. There are two "Mandarin Companion Universe" and two sci-fi easter eggs hidden in the illustrations of this book. Can you find them?

Cast of Characters

谢心月
(Xiè Xīnyuè)

马天明
(Mǎ Tiānmíng)

车老师
(Chē Lǎoshī)

方老师
(Fāng Lǎoshī)

水老师
(Shuǐ Lǎoshī)

Locations

山东 (Shāndōng)

Although not explicitly stated, this story takes place in a smallish city in China's Shandong Province.

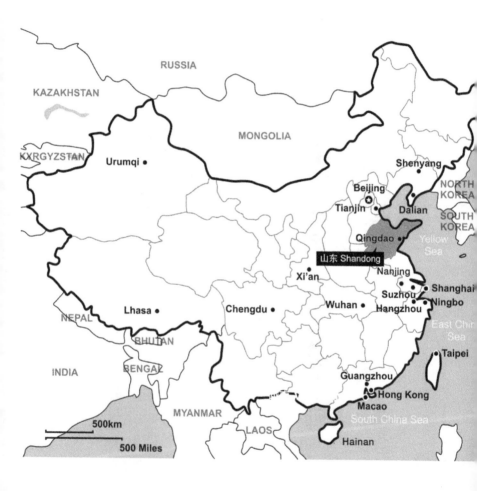

Chapter 1
外星人

谢心月 今年十岁，她是一个小学生。她有一个新朋友，叫"马天明"，马天明今年也是十岁。他们每天都一起去上学。

马天明 的爸爸今年已经四十岁了，他写过很多书，他的新书里有外星人，马天明 和谢心月 都会看他写的书。有时候，两个爸爸会和他们一起去山上看星星。

---

1 岁 (suì) *mw.* years old
2 小学生 (xiǎoxuéshēng) *n.* elementary school student
3 每天 (měitiān) *phrase* every day
4 上学 (shàngxué) *vo.* to go to school
5 已经 (yǐjing) *adv.* already
6 外星人 (wàixīngrén) *n.* alien
7 有时候 (yǒu shíhou) *phrase* sometimes, there are times
8 星星 (xīngxing) *n.* star, stars

"有很多星星，可是星星 太小了，

星星 上有外星人 吗？"马天明 问谢心月。

"我也不知道。我很想见见外星人！"

谢心月 说。

"你不怕 外星人 吗？"马天明 问。

You're not afraid of aliens?

---

9 怕 (pà) *v.* to be afraid (of)

"我不怕，你呢？"谢心月 说。

马天明 说："我也不怕。我爸爸说，外星人 在天上可以看见我们，可是，我们不能看见他们。"

Aliens can see us in sky

"我看了你爸爸写的新书，书里说了外星人 的样子。他是不是已经 见过外星人 了？"谢心月 问。

马天明 笑了："他没有见过外星人。"

He hasn't seen aliens

"你说，外星人 会说中文 吗？"谢心月 问。"要是 他们不会说中文，我们怎么和他们说话？"

马天明 想了想说："我不知道，可能他们可以。"

I don't know maybe they can

---

10 中文 (Zhōngwén) *n.* Chinese   12 可能 (kěnéng) *adv.* maybe
11 要是 (yàoshi) *conj.* if

"要是你见了一个会说中文的外星人，你会跟他说什么？"谢心月又问。

If you meet an alien who speaks chinese, you'll speak to them?

马天明有很多很多话想问外星人：“我……我要问他们，他们的家在什么地方，他们那里和我们这里有什么不一样，他们为什么要来我们这里……”

马爸爸听完以后就笑了。

to laugh

"明天星期一，又要上学了。不知道外星人小朋友是不是也都要上学？"谢心月说。

"见到外星人的时候，你就问他们吧。"马爸爸笑了笑。

---

13 地方 (dìfang) *n.* place
14 不一样 (bù yíyàng) *phrase* not the same
15 以后 (yǐhòu) *adv.* after

16 就 (jiù) *adv.* just
17 星期 (xīngqī) *n.* week
18 时候 (shíhou) *n.* when

— Chapter 2 —
车老师

第二天，来了一个小学老师，是男老师。"大家好，我是你们的新老师，你们可以叫我车老师，我今年三十岁。"

"车？我没有听过。"谢心月 说。

"我也没听过。"马天明 说，"车老师，你是哪里人？"

"我去过很多地方，你问我是哪里人，我不知道怎么说。"

老师的话有点好笑，学生们都笑了。

---

19 好笑 (hǎoxiào) *adj.* funny

车老师 看过很多星星 和火星 的书，每次 说到火星，他就 能说很多：知道火星 在哪里，火星 上没有水，也没有人……听车老师 说火星 的时候，马天明和谢心月 都很开心。

---

20 火星 (Huǒxīng) *pn.* Mars   21 每次 (měi cì) *phrase* every time

"老师，你的家不在火星上，怎么知道这么多？"谢心月 问。

"我爸爸的新书里也没写过这么多。"马天明 也说。

车老师 没说话，对他们笑笑。

有一天，学生和老师已经 都走了，马天明 和谢心月 回来 拿 东西。到门边的时候，他们看到车老师 在里面。他一边 用左手写字，一边 用右手写字，一边 看书！

"快看，车老师！怎么可能 ……"马天明 对谢心月 说。

谢心月 说："我看到了，这不是我第

---

22 回来 (huílai) *vc.* to come back
23 拿 (ná) *v.* to get, to hold
24 门边 (mén biān) *phrase* by the door
25 里面 (lǐmiàn) *n.* inside
26 一边 (yībiān) *conj.* while (doing)

一次看到他这样[27]了。”

马天明又说：“车老师是个什么人……”

“他会听到的，回家[28]说吧。”谢心月说。

27 这样 (zhèyàng) *pr.* like this
28 回家 (huíjiā) *vo.* to go home

第二天中午 吃饭的时候，马天明
对谢心月 说："我们快去问问他吧。他是
我们的老师，他是一个好老师。"

"你去问吧，我不想去。"谢心月 说。

马天明 笑笑："快去吧！车老师 是
很好的人。"

谢心月 想了想："好吧，车老师 一
个人在那儿吃饭。我们过去吧。"

— Chapter 3 —
他是人吗？

谢心月 和马天明 走到车老师 的后面，车老师 没有看到他们。

看到车老师 的饭很多，还没吃，谢心月 对马天明 说："老师的饭是不是不太好吃？我去拿 我们的饭来一起吃吧。"

她一边 说，一边 去拿 饭。

"我们不是来和老师吃饭的……"马天明 回头 叫她。

车老师 听到后面 有人，回头 看到了马天明。

---

30 后面 (hòumian) *n.* behind   31 回头 (huítóu) *vo.* to turn one's head

"老师好。"

"你吃饭了吗?"

"还没，我看到老师你也没吃……"马天明 的话没说完，车老师 的饭都已经吃完了！

这时候，谢心月 回来 了，手里拿的是她和马天明 的饭。

"我已经吃好了，你们吃吧。"车老师走的时候，对他们笑笑。

"这怎么可能……那么多饭，一下子都没了！"谢心月 说。可是马天明 也不知道，他们都不知道车老师 是怎么吃完的。

---

32 这时候 (zhè shíhou) *phrase* at this time

33 一下子 (yīxiàzi) *adv.* all at once

"车老师 是外星来的……"马天明
一边 吃一边 说。

"车老师 和我们一样，和我们说一
样的话，怎么可能 是外星人？"谢心月
说。

马天明 还在吃："可是，你也看到

了，他一边 用左手写字，一边 用右手
写字，一边 看书。我想他是外星人 吧。"

马天明 吃完了说："我也不知道。
要是 我们能到他家去看看，可能 会知
道为什么。你要不要一起去？"

"你知道车老师 的家在什么地方
吗？"谢心月 问。

马天明 说："我知道！"

谢心月 很开心："好，我和你一起
去。"

— Chapter 4 —
车老师的家

第二天下午五点，马天明 说："谢心月，我看见车老师 已经 走了。我们在他后面，要小心 一点，不要说话。"

"好的，我知道了。"

他们在车老师 后面 走了一个多小时，谢心月 问："马天明，这是去车老师家的路吗？ 怎么还没到……"

"这是车老师 回家 的路，快到车老师家了。"马天明 回头 对谢心月 说。

可是， 马天明 的话说完的时候，

---

34 小心 (xiǎoxīn) v. to be careful　　35 小时 (xiǎoshí) n. hour

车老师 就 不见了。

"人呢?怎么一下子 不见了?"马天明
说。

"车老师 是不是已经 看到我们了?
我们这样 不太好吧。"谢心月 听起来有
点不开心。

"他不可能 看到我们。我们小心 一
点,可能 他已经 到家了。你看,他的家
在前面。"马天明 说。

"家里没人……"到了车老师 家门边,
马天明 说。

"可能 他去朋友家了吧。我们明天
再来吧。"谢心月 说。

---

36 不见了 (bùjiàn le) *phrase*
disappeared

马天明 还是想看到车老师："再看看，可能 他还在路上。"

可是，一个小时 以后，车老师 还是没有回来。

"都七点了，我们回家 吧。"谢心月说。

"好，那我们明天再来。"

第三天下午，他们又 小心地 走在
了车老师 后面。可是，不知道怎么了，
车老师 在路上又 不见了。他们小心地
走到车老师 家，可是，他也没有回家。

后来，他们又在车老师 后面 走了
几次，每次 车老师 都不见了，也不在
他家里。车老师 每天 回家 以后 去了哪
里呢？

— Chapter 5 —
很大的星星

"马天明，我们这样 在车老师 后面 一个多星期 了，还是什么都不知道。"谢心月 说。

马天明 没听谢心月 说话："马上到车老师 家了，我们就 去他家门边 吧。"

这时候，谢心月 看看天，说："马天明，快看！这里有一个很大的星星！"

马天明 也看看天，说："怎么会这样？车老师 家上面 的天有这么大的星星……"

他们说话的时候，走到了车老师 家
          18

门边。
24

谢月心说："车老师 的家在大星星
                      8

的下面，可是车老师 不在家里。我们
   39

在他后面 这么多天，他每天 都不回家
   30   3   28

……"

---

39 下面 (xiàmian) *n.* below

马天明 还在看天。

"外星人 的家 不会在这里，可是……"不能开门去看，马天明 很不开心。"我想去看看。"

"你不怕 吗?"谢心月 说问。

"我不怕。"马天明 说。

"我也不怕。我可以叫我爸爸……来开这个门，他什么门都会开。"谢心月说。

"这样 不好。再说，我们还不知道车老师 是什么人，不能跟你爸爸说。"马天明 说。

"那我们能和谁说?"

"我们去跟方老师 说吧，车老师 家

的上面 有一个很大的星星，方老师 是一个好老师，可能 她会和我们来车老师的家看看。"

"好，那我们明天跟她说。"

— Chapter 6 —
方老师

第二天下午，谢心月 和马天明 问方老师："老师，你有没有去过车老师的家？"

"没去过，怎么了？"方老师 笑了一下，"大家都走了，你们两个怎么还不回家？"

"我们知道车老师 的家在哪儿。"谢心月 说。

"你能不能和我们一起去车老师 的家看看。"马天明 很小心地 说，他们三

个人可以听见。

方老师 想了想，说，"车老师 怎么了？你们为什么要去他家？"

"车老师 ……他不是人……"马天明说每一个字都很小心。

"你说什么？"方老师 听起来有点生气，"你是不是要说，车老师 不是一个好老师？"

"不是，他是一个好老师，可是，他和我们不一样。"马天明 说。

"有什么不一样？"方老师 问。

"他是火星 来的。"谢心月 不小心 跟方老师 说了。"我们在他后面 几次。可是，他在路上每次 都会一下子 不见了。"

---

40 生气 (shēngqì) vo. to get angry　　41 不小心 (bù xiǎoxīn) phrase to not be careful; accidentally

　　"我们每次 去他家，他都不在家。

你和我们一起去看看，好不好？"马天明

又说。

　　"他家上面 有一个星星，星星 也很

大。我们这里的天上没有，我家，马天明

家上面 也没有。"谢心月 又说。

"怎么会有那么大的星星？"方老师想。

"好吧。那我和你们去看看。"两个小朋友说的话有点好笑，可是，方老师还是去了。

到了车老师家门边，他们看见里面有人。

"车老师 在家……"谢心月 看看马天明。

"车老师 在家看书……怎么 可能……"马天明 看看谢心月，"他知道我们要来。"

谢心月 说："可是，他怎么会知道我们要来？"

马天明 又看看天："怎么会这样？天

上的大星星 没有了。”

　　“好了，我不知道你们两个在车老师

家看到过什么。可是，我看到车老师

在家，以后 不要再说他是火星人 了。”

方老师 有一点 生气，“快回家 吧。”

---

42 火星人 (Huǒxīng-rén) *pn.* Martian　　43 有一点 (yǒuyīdiǎn) *adv.* a little,
somewhat

— Chapter 7 —
本子

那天以后，马天明 和谢心月 就 不再去车老师 家了。可是，他们还是每天都在说车老师。

"马天明，我看到车老师 手里有一个本子，他每天 都在上面 写东西。"

"什么本子？"

"有一次，我们看到他一边 用左手写字，一边 用右手写字，一边 看书，对不对？写字的那个本子 和他每天 拿 的本子 是一样的。"

44 本子 (běnzi) *n.* notebook

"你看过那个本子 上写的东西吗?"
马天明 问。

"没有。那个本子 在他手里。我拿
不到那个本子，没有看过本子 里的字。"
谢心月 说。

"不用拿到那个本子，我们也可以看到。"马天明 笑了一下。

谢心月 很开心："那，本子 在哪里呢？"

马天明 想了想："听说，今天下午有很多老师不在，车老师 也可能 不在。他出去的时候，我们可以看看他的本子里面写了什么。"

"你说得对。"谢心月 说。

下午三点多的时候，车老师 出去了，他没有拿 那个本子。学生们有的在看书，有的在写字。

马天明 和谢心月 很开心，可是，他

---

45 拿到 (nádào) *w.* to get, to manage to get

们不想大家知道他们要去看老师的东
西。

"谢心月,"马天明一边叫他的朋友,
一边看车老师的本子。"我的本子在老
师那里,我去看看。"

"我的本子也在老师那里。"说完,

谢心月 和马天明 一起走了过去。

"这么多本子，哪个是我的?"谢心月
在看学生们的本子，马天明 在看车老师
的本子。

Chapter 8
不认识的字

车老师 的本子 上写了很多字，可是，马天明 不认识 本子 上的字。"你见过这样 的字吗?"马天明 说话的时候 很小心，不想大家听到。

"没见过。车老师 怎么会写这样 的字? 这会不会是外星人 的字?"

谢心月 拿 了几个学生的本子，可是，她看的是车老师 的本子。

"很有可能。"马天明 说。"我们都认识字。可是，他写外星人 的字，外星人 认识，我们不认识。"

46 认识 (rènshi) *v.* to recognize

谢心月 点点头，问："你看完了吗？
一会儿 车老师 回来 看到我们，他会不
开心的。"

"这是什么？"本子 上有一个人，这
个人的头里面 有一个人，心里面 还有
一个人。外星人 不好看，可是他们看起
来很开心。外星人 的手里还拿 了很多
东西。

"马天明！"谢心月 叫了出来。"快
看！怎么会有这样 的东西？"

"小心 一点，不要叫，也不要怕。"
马天明 说。

谢心月 小心地 说，"去跟方老师 说

吧。"

他们去见了方老师。方老师 看到了

他们，还看到了车老师 的本子。

方老师 说："你们怎么有车老师 的

本子？"

"方老师，车老师 的本子……里面

写的字我们都不认识，还有……你快看一下吧。"马天明 说。

"你们两个怎么还在说车老师？"方老师 拿 起那个本子，看了看，说："你们要我看什么？ 里面 什么都没有。"

"不可能！"马天明 和谢心月 一起

说。马天明 拿 起本子，说："我们都看到了，有很多外星人 的字，还有外星人在一个人里面……"

"怎么都没有了？怎么会这样……"
谢心月 有一点 不开心。

"你们两个，我也不知道说什么了。"
方老师 说。

— Chapter 9 —
车老师走了

一天中午 吃饭的时候，谢心月 问马天明："你说，车老师 是不是知道了？"

"有可能。"马天明 一边 吃饭，一边说。

又过了几个月，他们听说车老师 要走了，两个人都不太开心。他们都知道车老师 是外星人，可是，很多人都不知道。

"你说，车老师 为什么要走？"谢心月问马天明。

49 几个月 (jǐ gè yuè) *phrase* several months

马天明 想了想说:"车老师 想,可能
我们都知道他是外星人 了。"

"也有可能 是他要回火星 了吧。"
谢心月 笑了一下,"我也想和他一起去
火星 看看!"

马天明 说:"我想我们去了 火星

以后，就 不能回来 了。"
　　　15　　　16　　　　22

　　说完，两个人都笑了。

　　车老师 走的那天，谢心月 和马天明

拿到 了车老师 的那个本子。
　　45　　　　　　　　　　44

　　"这是我的本子，给你们吧。"车老师
　　　　　　　　　　　44

说。

马天明 和谢心月 一起说:"谢谢老师。"

车老师 很开心地说:"我还是你们的朋友。再见!"

马天明 和谢心月 不太开心:"老师再见!"

车老师 走的时候,谁都没有问他要去哪儿,以后 还会不会回来。

"马天明,本子 上写的东西都没了。"谢心月 看完以后 说。

— Chapter 10 —
水老师

车老师 走了以后 的第二年，又来
了一个新的男老师。

"大家好，我是水老师，今年三十
二岁。"男老师说，"我是你们今年的新老
师，很开心认识 大家。"

"水？"一个男生笑了，"我没听过。"

"我想，下一个 老师会叫火老师。"
马天明 也笑了。大家听他这样 说，也
都笑了。

马天明 和谢心月 没想到的是，水老师

50 下一个 (xià yī ge) *phrase* next one

和车老师 一样，也看过很多星星 和火星

的书。每次 说到火星，水老师 也会说

很多。

　　"水老师，你知道吗？"谢心月 说，"去

年我们有一个车老师。他和你一样，每次

说到火星，也会说很多。"

"水老师，你可能 不认识 他。"马天明说。"他……很不一样。"

"怎么不一样？"水老师 一边 笑一边问。

"他很喜欢星星，很喜欢火星。"马天明说。

"我也是 !"水老师 说。"我认识 车老师。他是我的好朋友。"

"真的？ 那，你也是火星人？"马天明问。

水老师 说："他和我说过你们。他说你们喜欢去他家，说你们也喜欢看他的本子。"

"他都知道 !"谢心月 说。

"你们还有他的本子 吗？"水老师
问。

"你要这个本子 吗？"马天明 不开
心。

"我不要。"水老师 说。"车老师 已经
给你们了。"

"可是本子 上面 没有字了！"谢心月
说。

"以后 会有的。"车老师 说。"会有
的。"

Key Words 关键词 (Guānjiàncí)

1. 岁 (suì) *mw.* years old
2. 小学生 (xiǎoxuéshēng) *n.* elementary school student
3. 每天 (měitiān) *phrase* every day
4. 上学 (shàngxué) *vo.* to go to school
5. 已经 (yǐjing) *adv.* already
6. 外星人 (wàixīngrén) *n.* alien
7. 有时候 (yǒu shíhou) *phrase* sometimes, there are times
8. 星星 (xīngxing) *n.* star, stars
9. 怕 (pà) *v.* to be afraid (of)
10. 中文 (Zhōngwén) *n.* Chinese
11. 要是 (yàoshi) *conj.* if
12. 可能 (kěnéng) *adv.* maybe
13. 地方 (dìfang) *n.* place
14. 不一样 (bù yīyàng) *phrase* not the same
15. 以后 (yǐhòu) *adv.* after
16. 就 (jiù) *adv.* just
17. 星期 (xīngqī) *n.* week
18. 时候 (shíhou) *n.* when
19. 好笑 (hǎoxiào) *adj.* funny
20. 火星 (Huǒxīng) *pn.* Mars
21. 每次 (měi cì) *phrase* every time
22. 回来 (huílai) *vc.* to come back
23. 拿 (ná) *v.* to get, to hold
24. 门边 (mén biān) *phrase* by the door
25. 里面 (lǐmiàn) *n.* inside
26. 一边 (yībiān) *conj.* while (doing)
27. 这样 (zhèyàng) *pr.* like this
28. 回家 (huíjiā) *vo.* to go home
29. 中午 (zhōngwǔ) *n.* noon
30. 后面 (hòumian) *n.* behind

31. 回头 (huítóu) *vo.* to turn one's head

32. 这时候 (zhè shíhou) *phrase* at this time

33. 一下子 (yīxiàzi) *adv.* all at once

34. 小心 (xiǎoxīn) *v.* to be careful

35. 小时 (xiǎoshí) *n.* hour

36. 不见了 (bùjiàn le) *phrase* disappeared

37. 小心地 (xiǎoxīn de) *phrase* carefully

38. 上面 (shàngmian) *n.* above

39. 下面 (xiàmian) *n.* below

40. 生气 (shēngqì) *vo.* to get angry

41. 不小心 (bù xiǎoxīn) *phrase* to not be careful; accidentally

42. 火星人 (Huǒxīng-rén) *pn.* Martian

43. 有一点 (yǒuyīdiǎn) *adv.* a little, somewhat

44. 本子 (běnzi) *n.* notebook

45. 拿到 (nádào) *vc.* to get, to manage to get

46. 认识 (rènshi) *v.* to recognize

47. 点点头 (diǎndian tóu) *vo.* to (briefly) nod one's head

48. 一会儿 (yīhuìr) *phrase* a little while

49. 几个月 (jǐ gè yuè) *phrase* several months

50. 下一个 (xià yī ge) *phrase* next one

Part of Speech Key

adj. Adjective

adv. Adverb

aux. Auxiliary Verb

conj. Conjunction

cov. Coverb

mw. Measure word

n. Noun

on. Onomatopoeia

part. Particle

prep. Preposition

pr. Pronoun

pn. Proper noun

tn. Time Noun

v. Verb

vc. Verb plus complement

vo. Verb plus object

Discussion Questions
讨论问题 (Tǎolùn Wèntí)

Chapter 1 外星人

1. 马爸爸的书里写了什么？

2. 你喜欢看星星吗？你觉得星星上有外星人吗？

3. 要是你见了一个会说英文的外星人，你会跟他说什么？

Chapter 2 车老师

1. 车老师是哪里人？

2. 车老师为什么知道火星在哪里？

3. 马天明和谢心月看到了什么？

Chapter 3 他是人吗？

1. 马天明为什么说车老师是外星人？

2. 你觉得车老师是外星人吗？为什么？

3. 马天明和谢心月为什么要去车老师家看看？

Chapter 4 车老师的家

1. 车老师在路上不见了，你觉得车老师去了哪里？

2. 你觉得车老师知道马天明和谢心月跟在他后面吗？为什么？

3. 你觉得车老师的家里有什么？

Chapter 5 很大的星星

1. 你觉得那个大星星上面有什么？

2. 马天明为什么不开心？

3. 你想去车老师的家里看看吗？

Chapter 6 方老师

1. 方老师去过车老师家吗?

2. 方老师为什么和他们去车老师家?

3. 方老师和他们去车老师家看到了什么?

Chapter 7 本子

1. 他们还去车老师家吗?

2. 他们为什么想看车老师的本子?

3. 他们想怎么看到那个本子?

Chapter 8 不认识的字

1. 车老师的本子上有什么?

2. 方老师看到本子上的字了吗?

3. 你想一想,为什么本子上的字没有了?

Chapter 9 车老师走了

1. 大家知道车老师是外星人吗?

2. 你想一想,为什么车老师要走呢?

3. 车老师给了他们什么?

Chapter 10 水老师

1. 新来的老师叫什么名字?

2. 新来的老师认识车老师吗?

3. 你想一想,新来的老师是外星人吗?

Appendix A:
Character Comparison Reference

This appendix is designed to help Chinese teachers and learners use the Mandarin Companion graded readers as a companion to the most popular university textbooks and the HSK word lists.

The tables below compare the characters and vocabulary used in other study materials with those found in this Mandarin Companion graded reader. The tables below will display the exact characters and vocabulary used in this book and not covered by these sources. A learner who has studied these textbooks will likely find it easier to read this graded reader by focusing on these characters and words.

Integrated Chinese Level 1, Part 1 (3rd Ed.)

Words and characters in this story not covered by these textbooks:

Character	Pinyin	Word(s)	Pinyin
心	xīn	心 开心 小心 心里	xīn kāixīn xiǎoxīn xīnli
马	mǎ	马 马上	Mǎ mǎshàng
山	shān	山上	shānshàng
怕	pà	不怕 怕	bù pà pà
又	yòu	又	yòu
完	wán	完 说完	wán shuōwán
拿	ná	拿 拿到	ná nádào
本	běn	本子	běnzi
火	huǒ	火星 火	Huǒxīng huǒ

Character	Pinyin	Word(s)	Pinyin
次	cì	每次 第一次 几次 次	měi cì dì-yī cì jǐ cì cì
门	mén	门边 开门 门	mén-biān kāimén mén
左	zuǒ	左手	zuǒshǒu
右	yòu	右手	yòushǒu
头	tóu	回头 点点头 头	huítóu diǎndian tóu tóu

New Practical Chinese Reader, Book 1 (1st Ed.)

Words and characters in this story not covered by these textbooks:

Character	Pinyin	Word(s)	Pinyin
已	yǐ	已经	yǐjīng
山	shān	山上	shānshàng
笑	xiào	笑 好笑 笑笑	xiào hǎoxiào xiàoxiao
又	yòu	又	yòu
地	de	地方 地	dìfang de
完	wán	完 说完	wán shuōwán
后	Hòu	以后 后面 后来	yǐhòu hòumiàn hòulái
就	jiù	就	jiù
边	biān	一边	yībiān

Character	Pinyin	Word(s)	Pinyin
		门边	mén-biān
火	huǒ	火星	Huǒxīng
		火	huǒ
走	zǒu	走	zǒu
门	mén	门边	mén-biān
		开门	kāimén
		门	mén
左	zuǒ	左手	zuǒshǒu
手	shǒu	左手	zuǒshǒu
		右手	yòushǒu
		手里	shǒulǐ
右	yòu	右手	yòushǒu
路	lù	路	lù
		路上	lùshang

Hanyu Shuiping Kaoshi (HSK) Levels 1-2

Words and characters in this story not covered by these levels:

Character	Pinyin	Word(s)	Pinyin
心	xīn	心	xīn
		开心	kāixīn
		小心	xiǎoxīn
		心里	xīnli
马	mǎ	马	mǎ
		马上	mǎshàng
山	shān	山上	shānshàng
怕	pà	不怕	bù pà
		怕	pà
文	Wén	中文	Zhōngwén

Character	Pinyin	Word(s)	Pinyin
跟	gēn	跟	gēn
又	yòu	又	yòu
地	de	地方 地	dìfang de
方	fāng	地方 方	dìfang fāng
拿	ná	拿 拿到	ná nádào
用	yòng	用 不用	yòng bùyòng
头	tóu	回头 点点头 头	huítóu diǎndian tóu tóu

Appendix B: Grammar Point Index

For learners new to reading Chinese, an understanding of grammar points can be extremely helpful for learners and teachers. The following is a list of the most challenging grammar points used in this graded reader.

These grammar points correspond to the Common European Framework of Reference for Languages (CEFR) level B1 or above. The full list with explanations and examples of each grammar point can be found on the Chinese Grammar Wiki, the definitive source of information on Chinese grammar online.

CHAPTER 1	
The "all" adverb "dou"	都 + Verb / Adj.
Tag questions with "ma"	······是吗 / 对吗 / 好吗?
Reduplication of verbs	Verb + Verb
After a specific time with "yihou"	Time / Verb + 以后
Expressing "if... then..." with "yaoshi"	要是······，就······
Expressing a learned skill with "hui"	会 + Verb
The "also" adverb "ye"	也 + Verb / Adj.
Expressing "will" with "hui"	会 + Verb
How to do something with "zenme"	怎么 + Verb？
Expressing "when" with "de shihou"	······的时候
Two words for "but"	······，可是 / 但是······
CHAPTER 2	
Suggestions with "ba"	Command + 吧
Expressing location with "zai... shang / xia / li"	在 + Place + 上 / 下 / 里 / 旁边
Simultaneous tasks with "yibian"	一边 + Verb 1 (,) 一边 + Verb 2
Using "dui" with verbs	Subj. + 对 + Person + Verb
CHAPTER 3	

Expressing "all at once" with "yixiazi"	Subj. + 一下子 + Verb + 了
Expressing "and" with "he"	Noun 1 + 和 + Noun 2
Expressing ability or possibility with "neng"	能 + Verb
Basic comparisons with "yiyang"	Noun 1 + 跟 / 和 + Noun 2 + 一样 + Adj.

CHAPTER 4

Expressing "again" in the future with "zai"	再 + Verb
Expressing "then…" with "name"	那么 ······
Expressing duration with "le"	Verb + 了 + Duration
Sequencing past events with "houlai"	······，后来 ······

CHAPTER 5

Expressing "everything" with "shenme dou"	什么 + 都 / 也 ······
Expressing "in addition" with "zaishuo"	······，再说，······
Expressing "with" with "gen"	跟 ······ + Verb
Causative verbs	Subj. + 让 / 叫 / 请 / 使 + Person + Predicate

CHAPTER 6

There are no new grammar points in this chapter.

CHAPTER 7

There are no new grammar points in this chapter.

CHAPTER 8

There are no new grammar points in this chapter.

CHAPTER 9

There are no new grammar points in this chapter.

CHAPTER 10

There are no new grammar points in this chapter.

Other Stories from Mandarin Companion

Breakthrough Readers: 150 Characters

Zhou Haisheng 《周海生》 by John Pasden, Jared Turner

Young Sherlock Xiao Ming 《小明》 by John Pasden, Jared Turner

In Search of Hua Ma 《花马》 by John Pasden, Jared Turner

Good Friends and Her 《好朋友和她》 by John Pasden, Jared Turner

Level 1 Readers: 300 Characters

The Secret Garden 《秘密花园》 by Frances Hodgson Burnett

The Sixty Year Dream 《六十年的梦》 by Washington Irving (based on *Rip Van Winkle*)

The Monkey's Paw 《猴爪》 by W. W. Jacobs

The Country of the Blind 《盲人国》 by H. G. Wells

Sherlock Holmes and the Case of the Curly-Haired Company 《卷发公司的案子》 by Sir Arthur Conan Doyle (based on *The Red Headed League*)

The Prince and the Pauper 《王子和穷孩子》 by Mark Twain

Emma 《安末》 by Jane Austen

The Ransom of Red Chief 《红猴的价格》 by O. Henry

Level 2 Readers: 450 Characters

Great Expectations: Part 1 《美好的前途（上）》 by Charles Dickens

Great Expectations: Part 2 《美好的前途（下）》 by Charles Dickens

Journey to the Center of the Earth 《地心游记》 by Jules Verne

Mandarin Companion is producing a growing library of
graded readers for Chinese language learners.

Visit our website for the newest books available:

www.MandarinCompanion.com

CPSIA information can be obtained
at www.ICGtesting.com
Printed in the USA
BVHW062142110320
574764BV00002B/34